THE SPRINGFEST SPRINT

FAETALES NOVELLA #1

POPPY MINNIX

ONE NIGHT READS

DEDICATION

You need a breather from big books.
You need to get out of a book slump.
You need to see if you like romantasy.
This is for you.
But also for me, because authors hit book slumps, too.
Enjoy my cure.
Love,
Poppy

INTRODUCTION

Note: In 2025 Poppy Minnix absorbed her alternate pen name Georgie Monroe (original author). The Faetales series will continue under Poppy Minnix

Hello lovers of fantasy and spice!

Welcome to the Faetale world!

This romantasy is a short story (2-hour average for reading) and has darker themes with high spice levels. (Look away if you don't like trigger warnings!)...

...

...

Last chance...

If you're not up for reading about a forced bonding/mating event, sexual descriptions, polyamory, assault situations (not from the hero), etc, this is your warning!

Happy reading!

Poppy

TOO TIGHT

EMBER

"Too tight," I wheeze as the race matron ties my bindings—a wicked web of straps. Despite her frail appearance from being five gajillion moons old, she's as strong as a beefy minotaur.

She crushes my wings tighter against my back. "Is not."

"Is. How am I expected to run if I can't breathe properly?"

Tighter.

"Mamaw, if you break my wings, I'll bite yours off."

She slaps my bare ass hard enough to make me yelp. "You'll be too busy running for that. Gentry Aspen has publicly stated his intentions." Another few slight tugs at the bindings and she lets me go. "It's a wonderful thing to be wanted by a gentry, though his friends will try to win you first."

His competitive frenemies. "Yeah, I'm aware." Mother was too happy to throw that information in my face.

"Then be aware of this." Mamaw's tone is hard beyond her constant state of grumpiness. Worry, maybe? When I turn to look at her, she grips my chin. The foggy green color of her eyes turns to clear dark blue. "Run. Do not play with them or get overconfident, Ember. Run far and fast, cover your tracks, and hide until your favorite comes near or at the least, get a group to fight for you and see who's the strongest mate. You deserve that much."

The strongest *mate*. My mouth goes dry because I'm not ready. "Why do we do this again?"

Her round blue wings open and close with her inhale, and she lets my chin go so she can braid a wide chunk of my hair. "Tradition, as you know. Culture. Those things that make us who we are and keep us aware of our past. Just like the Equinox Festival and the Guardian Ceremony, we have the Springfest Sprint in the middle of our most blessed season." Tugging a braid, she turns me to her and taps my nose. "You are of binding age and haven't chosen, so you must be bound to the one who conquers you."

I lift my clenched jaw. "Unless they don't conquer me."

"If anyone can find her freedom, it's you. I bet you know our territory better than Gentry Aspen." That's a compliment. Few get compared to the highest ranking position in the fae armies. "You've tested every boundary ward since you could flutter. And maybe you've been training, yes?" She smiles, damn well knowing I have, because I swear she uses some ancient magic to stick her eyes and ears into places they shouldn't be.

I can't lie, not that it matters in this case. No matter what I've done to undermine my role in this traditional event, I still have to take part. So I remain quiet while Mamaw finishes my hair, then leads me to the preparation room with the other runners. Silks fly around like exploding dandelion fluff, draping over curves and bound wings.

There are ten of us running and eight hunting. That's good for me, if I can hide and Gentry Aspen gives up, which he won't.

It's not that I don't like him—he's a good male—but I don't like how he kisses. It's wet. Like pressing my lips against a moss bed after a rainstorm. Slobber just squishes out, which is why three moons ago, I made an excuse after five minutes of making out and flew into the night. And now, according to him, I'm playing hard to get. Hopefully, he'll accept my disappearing act because I won't kiss soaked moss for the rest of my days. Someone here will love his power and gold more than his drowning lips, but that fae is not me.

"Who are you hoping for, Em?" Storm asks, accepting a dusting of moth glimmer from a hovering pixie. Her twin Rain appears ready to pass out, not only from the bindings. She's breathing fast and frowning, fingers jittering over straps. Storm holds her other hand; always the protector.

Rounds of "Yeah, who?" come from the others.

I tap my pursed lips. Clay maybe, though that may be awkward after my fling with his sister, which was so, so good. That did not totally thrill him, so maybe not Clay, even if I'm curious about his lanky body and how he's been too shy and sweet to pursue me for anything more than conversation, but is ready to claim one of us. *Publicly.* My head spins with thoughts of the hunters I've known all my life and I honestly can't pick, because I don't want any of them in the forever way. There's so much to see, do, and discover on my own. What about the next time the autumn fae come to visit? I'll be on the arm of my *mate*, not flirting and dancing with others. Unable to sneak off and fulfill fantasies with no pressure because my temporary lover would leave within a few days. They wouldn't seek to tie me down—into a relationship.

I'm not ready for this. I shrug. "No one. I'm running for it."

Chapter Two

The Hunters

EMBER

I've had years to wrap my mind around this event, yet I can't believe I'm here, getting ready to attempt to thwart my fate. The diaphanous blue silks I'm wrapped in cover my breasts and bindings on my top half. More are tied low on my hips, draping too long, mostly hiding the bareness between my legs and also my backside. It's something I'd love to wear any day I'm not required to run from a pack of male fae who only need to exhale to uncover my girly goods and end my freedom. I have one veto and three hunters I'd use it on. I could plead for them not to take me, but Gentry Aspen wouldn't listen—he's really set on that playing-hard-to-get thing he believes I'm doing. Nor would Basil—he certainly didn't listen to what would have made me come when we spent a night together. And then there's Jasper, Gentry Aspen's second-in-command, who wouldn't heed my request to spite the other two. Those three are exactly the mates I want to avoid.

Guards herd us like fish down a narrow stream through the life tree's lower corridor. At least I'm in front. I glance back at Quartz, who glares at me. Her hair is slightly disheveled from my tug a few moments ago.

I smile at her. "You're right. This spot is fantastic; good luck to you too."

She remains unamused.

As soon as we reach the exit, my wings twitch to flutter. I could be in the air in seconds. Instead, I'm on two feet—a massive disadvantage. Not only will I be slower, but I'll have fewer hiding places and less ability to maneuver. The males will not. But it's clear the Springfest Sprint isn't meant to have winners.

I get it, unfortunately. We need children, and if we're bound, we're more likely to go into heat and produce the next generations to defend our borders. But still. Maybe if I win, I can do the unthinkable and ask to visit the summer court to meet others and then the autumn court after that, getting in both travel and ambassador-level meet and greets. I can make the excuse that it's to study their traditions.

As the gathered crowd cheers and the hunters come into view, I realize my thoughts of escape are merely daydreams.

The males are decorated with nature to make them stealthier, as well as a small cloth covering their dicks, many of which are lifted by erections, fully prepared to win their hunted mate as quickly as possible. Wings of all shapes and sizes are open, slowly moving in the gentle breeze.

Mine twitch again, wishing to be as free.

Jasper points at me, skin painted with streaks of charcoal, making him into a beautiful shadow, perfect for hunting. I really wish he wasn't such a pompous bore. He rumbles, "Mine."

I roll my eyes at him.

Gentry Aspen shoves his second's hand down and sets his own fist over his heart, bowing his head as if his pledge should comfort me. He's wearing gray feathers and ash paints a pale, speckled mask on his face. He lifts his head and grins at me.

My stomach twists as I think about all the slobber.

The other males mumble, laugh, and stare down their intended prey, many of their gazes landing on me and then flitting over the crowd to find my mother on the throne.

She gives me a nod, but her eyes remain cold. Still angry with me for not choosing the gentry when I had the chance, I see.

There's a pop of magic behind me and I spin. An image of myself stands where Storm had been. She must want Gentry Aspen. It's an impressive glamour—one she's clearly been practicing. My braids look fabulous, but she didn't quite get the mischief in my eyes right.

I smile at her and I smile back. That makes me giggle. The males would know her scent the moment they're on her, but maybe they'll be too caught up to care. She'd make a better mate than I would, anyway.

Mother stands, her iridescent wings pointed high and wide. The excited crowd falls silent. "The Springfest Sprint shall commence in fifty flutters. Release the hunted."

Chapter Three

RUNNING FOR MY STRIFE

EMBER

With my mother's announcement, I start out at a slow pace past the attentive hunters.

The other prey fall behind me like I've started a human jogging club. When we squish together to enter the rocky ravine, and females crunch together, arguing for more space, I'm even more appreciative that I shoved my way to the front.

As soon as we pass through, I yell, "Good fortune to those who wish for it," and dash left toward the river, listening to the others mumble and stamp noisily in all directions. Twenty flutters into my sprint, silk tangles around my quick legs and I halt too late, tumbling to the forest floor with a screech as my wings try desperately to break free. "We're not meant for running," I grumble, staggering to my feet. Especially not in too-long panels of silk.

My knees leak crimson, and I shake my head. Bleeding will not help me hide. I need to get to the water. Tying the silk panels together, I fashion something close to a silky diaper—maybe that will deter them as well—and get back to my escape plan. Has it been forty flutters or forty-five? I finally find what I'm looking for, leaping from rock to rock as I close in on the river.

Some don't pay attention to our territory, trusting the work of the gentry and army, but I've studied these woods and this stream until it formed a detailed map in my mind. Now, I move closer to what I can only hope will hide me well enough for the others to be claimed first. It's definitely been fifty flutters, and I waver between sticking to the trees and underbrush so I have coverage or dashing along the rocks so my steps are silent.

A distant scream stops me in my tracks, and then a jumble of yelling takes over.

I run with renewed fervor, sticking to the coverage of trees, because whatever scuffle is unfolding won't last long enough.

A buzz of wings sounds and I throw myself against a tree, trying desperately to ease my heaving lungs. The sound halts, and a tree branch creaks to my right. This is where someone who was panicking would run, but I'd be caught four steps into a sprint.

I dig my fingers into the bark and slowly blow out the air from my burning lungs.

There's another buzz, and for a moment, I hope they've flown away, but one speaks.

"Have you seen Quartz?" Stone has to be only a tree over. Too close.

"Nah. My eyes are set for one." Jasper's voice makes me grit my teeth. *Go, please. Leave.*

"That little tart is trouble, and you know it." Stone's voice is quietly conspiratorial.

Hey. I cut my eyes in his direction, but don't dare to move.

Jasper chuckles. "It's worth it."

I roll my eyes. That says a lot. Not *she's worth it*, but *it*—my title and status. That's all Jasper has ever been interested in.

"Well, I doubt the little princess would have made it this far already, nor would she come here. Too close to mud and stream muck for her precious self."

I can count myself fortunate that Stone isn't interested, though it's hard for me to stay still instead of turning around and giving him the what for, the peephole.

"You're probably right. Maybe she's in the fields." Jasper gives a disgruntled hum, and two sets of wings flutter off.

I rescind the peephole insult. Stone can lure Jasper away anytime.

Keeping still and calm for another long moment, I listen to the sounds of the forest: birds, distant buzzing, and there are definitely moans coming from the west. Two are out of the game, it seems.

Pushing off the tree, I step into a run, wincing at the slight crunch of last year's plant remains between the clumps of fresh growth. The creek comes into sight and I grin. Then I screech as I'm tackled, landing hard amongst a bed of daffodils.

Chapter Four

NOT THIS ETERNITY

EMBER

My tackler pins me face down and runs his nose up my neck as I struggle to turn around.

My skin prickles and my lady parts shrivel up and hide. If only that were possible. "Let go." I land an elbow hard enough to make him hiss.

"Not a chance." Jasper's tone is amusement. "I knew you were hiding. Could feel you."

"What does that even mean?"

"You're a magic creature." He grips my knee and tugs.

I kick him away. "So are you."

"You have potent energy."

Which is why I haven't used magic yet. Anyone close by would feel it, and if I can get away quietly, I may still stick to my plan. I shove his hand away from my breast. "Look. I'm not interested in being claimed. Just back away and we'll go our separate ways."

"That's not how the game is played and you know it. What in snail's spit is this?" He tugs at my knotted silks but I twist to make it more difficult to untie. "I'll get it," he growls. "Then I'll have bragging rights for decades. And the court in my pocket." His rumble of a laugh sends rage through me.

At least Gentry Aspen seems to like me.

I sigh. "Oh, well. Guess I'm caught then." I relax and wait, hoping this works.

"Very good, Ember. I'm the best choice here."

He probably actually thinks that. He rolls me to my back and sits up, giving me the perfect chance to kick him in the face, which I do. As hard as I can.

Then I'm up and hauling myself through the forest, backtracking to get to the thorn grove, where he would have a hard time navigating without ripping up his wings. Since mine are bound, they're somewhat protected.

The tackle this time is harder, and I cry out.

"That was unkind," Jasper growls.

"So is taking me when I don't want you." I punch at him, but he gathers my wrists, pushing them against my chest.

"You don't want anyone. But that doesn't matter because I'm the one who got to you first." He taps the medallion on his chest, calling out to his designated referee. "Now, hold still."

"Like Arawn, I will." I struggle to evade his every attempt to untie my silks. "Don't make me use my veto."

He pauses, brown eyes wide. "You wouldn't."

Staring back, I call to the magics, gathering them in my chest. "I would. I won't be bound to someone who only wants to use my station and to brag. Do you know how terrible that is to hear?"

He looks cowed—embarrassed even, yet tries for my silks again. This event brings out the competition to a cruel level, but also exposes the most candid side of the hunters and the hunted. It brings out the things we skillfully hide because we're used to having a moment to think through words and actions.

As we both struggle, there's no time to think.

I let the magic snap into place. It's a tiny glamour—hopefully not enough for anyone to feel past a foot.

Jasper screams and jumps back.

I scramble backwards and up.

He drags me down again. "You think some maggots on your face are going to deter me?"

"I'd—" I shove at him. Kick. "Hoped." I'm free for a second, then pinned again.

A throat clears, and Willow hovers above us, looking like a floating candle with her fiery hair and gray outfit. "I'm here to witness the bonding." I wonder if this event hurts for her. She lost her mate three seasons back—one she loved and chose before the Springfest Sprint.

"Give me one moment," Jasper says, ripping my silks apart.

"Veto," I yell, dropping my glamour. "I invoke my veto."

Jasper curses as he's yanked off of me and held by the invisible hand of magic Willow yields.

She smiles at me with sad, kind eyes. "Are you sure? Jasper is—" she looks over him. "Strong and handsome."

I stand, panting and retying what's left of my skirt. "That he is." I check the scratches on my arms and legs, noting the disaster of mud and flower stains I've become, and try to pull two twigs from my braids. They're stuck good, though, and probably look like horns. I leave them. Maybe someone will think I'm a tiny deer and leave me be. Walking toward my original path, I pat Jasper's firm backside. "No hard feelings, but I'm going to pass on being a memento mate you use for political gain. Good luck with whoever."

"Maybe me?" a voice calls from behind us.

It's me. Or Storm still holding the glamour of me. So she was after Jasper, not Gentry Aspen. That's both amusing and terrible because that means I still have to deal with another.

"You want me?" Jasper asks, confused.

"For like ever, you dolt. Did me saying, 'I want this forever,' the times we came together not sink in?" I smile—or *she* smiles. "I can even hold the glamour if that does it for you."

"Wow." I cringe. "Okay then. Hoorah? Whatever. Congratulations, I think." I take off toward my hiding spot.

Chapter Five

The Best Little Hiding Space Around. Unfortunately.

Ember

I dash through the river, watching the skies and checking behind me every two flutters.

There's a ruckus from the north that's a little too close, and I run harder, not worrying about the noise because it's masked well enough. A wave of clover-tasting magic surges through the air. That was a hunter—Basil, or maybe Leaf.

I scrunch my nose. If someone just got fried, Mother will be a beast until the next moon.

The sludge is difficult to navigate, but I stay in the stream. I'm not leaving tracks, and the water washes away the blood from my cuts and scraped knees. I punch a minnow that tries to taste my foot and stumble, yipping, and then covering my mouth.

"Greetings, Ember."

Screeching from behind my palm, I spin. Clay perches on a rock, looking me up and down.

I pull a loose silk back up over my shoulder. "Hi."

He didn't tackle me. That's a good start. He's braided his soft black hair into rows, and knotted them on the back of his head. He's lanky, even for a faery, but with defined muscle and little dark nipples I imagine licking.

I step toward him. He's far better than the others, I think. I'm not ready to settle, but are any of us? I could see myself with Clay, though. Hopefully, the made-your-sister-scream-in-ecstasy thing won't be too much of a problem for us. The people of my court are possessive.

"I wanted to ask you—" He licks his thick bottom lip and doesn't leave strings of drool behind *and* he's asking? That's enough criteria for a wedding. He'll look dapper in a gray suit to match his eyes.

"Yes?" I smile and take another step closer.

Brows furrowed, he tilts his head, leaning away from me. "Have you seen Rain?"

I pause my apparent intrusion into his space. "Rain? Timid, not me, Rain?"

He nods. "Yes."

"Wow, I really read that wrong." I take a step back and wipe my dirty hands on my filthy silks. "I haven't seen her. But Storm and Jasper may be a thing now and were last seen near the thorn grove. If anyone knows where she's hiding, it's her twin."

He leaps into the air. "Good luck, Ember. I hope you find what you seek."

I seek nothing. "You too. Don't tell anyone you saw me." I watch my only choice fly off with a quickness. "Huh." That stung. And I should probably keep my head in the game. I get back to running the river and punching minnows until the stones become bigger and more abundant. Perfect. Now this is a hideout.

Winding through the maze of boulders is far easier than running, and every sound—from seed pods clacking together to cricket chirps—bounces off the stone, echoes a sweet song of aloneness. The nervous knot in my chest loosens, and I breathe as deeply and fully as I can with my wings bound. Here I will wait. I lean into a rocky nook. Not the most comfortable hammock ever, but I'll live. It will only be a few hours... I think. They'll give up and find the others. I should have probably grabbed a berry or four to tide me over until the feast.

With a sharp clack, a beak pecks just left of my hip.

I roll away from the attack, glaring up at the starling aiming for me again. "I am not a bug, you horrid be—"

The next peck would stab through my forehead if I didn't drop between the rocks. Balling my fingers, I focus to prevent releasing a lightning ball that would spill feathers as the seed-brain startled but possibly be a beacon to my hiding spot. Looks like I'm not getting any sunshine or fresh air while I wait out the hunt.

Following the narrow maze downward, I drop onto a solid dirt ground that rumbles with the sounds of water underneath. I like this little cave. I'm not sure anyone else knows of it since no one has mentioned its discovery, but if I'm lucky, they're not like me. I didn't want to share the quiet solitude, and calm pool that's tucked into the corner. It's hard for my eyes to adjust to such little light, but I follow my feet to the edge of the pool and tug at the top straps of my silks. How long would they take to dry if I washed them here?

There's a hum in the dark, then a deep chuckle as I look around, trying to see into the shadows.

"You look rather rough, tiny Fae."

To Hecate with the magic push, I launch a light ball toward the amused, unfamiliar voice.

CHAPTER SIX

THE BAD GUY

EMBER

The male catches my light ball.

It takes me a moment to fully register what he just did. Who catches light balls? No one, that's who.

The stranger stares at it in his palm, turning it this way and that, highlighting his face and defined shoulders. "Now that's new." His features are pale and chiseled—hauntingly sexy. And he's in my pond—a pile of clothing and a large satchel haphazardly thrown nearby in the moss.

I touch a toe into the water, but it's still warm. If a winter fae has snuck past our borders to bring a late, debilitating frost, my people may call off the hunt to deal with it. "If you're planning on making my pond into an ice-skating rink, we're going to have a problem." One that may solve my Springfest Sprint problem, but he doesn't need to know that.

He tilts his head, pointed ear poking out of his wet, light ash hair. "Ice skating?"

"Winter fae? It's not your season anymore."

"I'm not a winter fae." He presses my light ball to the wall where a tree root curls around it. "Let me guess, tiny Seelie. Hm." Lifting his chin, he inhales, lids fluttering closed. That is the sexiest smirk. "Spring fae?"

"Obviously. What court are you from, then? And don't call me 'tiny.'" I've thrown Jasper for that. More than once.

The light ball stays lit like a wall sconce. How? I want to do that.

He stands until the water kisses his hip muscles and walks closer, stepping out of the water and—my goddess—he's tall and thick and wow. His manhood is an impressive thing, not standing up enough for me to see the full size when hard, but threatening to.

I can just make out the bottom of his wings. They look... jagged? Must be the shadows.

He stands in front of me, and I'm at eye level with his nipples. They're better than Clay's—pink and tight enough for me to get my teeth around them just right. "But you are so tiny." The way he speaks makes his lips move nimbly—like they were made to draw attention to every word. Magic, maybe? Is it glamour? He walks around me, and oddly, it doesn't feel like a threat.

However, the energy pouring from him makes my skin tingle.

He grips a ripped panel of my silks and massages the fabric between his fingers and thumb. "Tiny and disheveled. What happened?"

"Just out for a roll in the fields, as we do..." During the Springfest Sprint. It's not a lie. I turn toward him, trying to get a glimpse of his wing shape, but he steps behind me and presses a soft touch between my shoulder blades, the center point between my wings. It feels like a direct button to my clit, and it takes a lot of concentration not to swoon backwards onto his cock. Has no one touched me there before? I can't remember, so even if they did, it didn't feel like this.

"You're trussed up." His breath tickles my neck and sends my skin into a shimmy. "Why are you trussed up?"

"Why are you asking?" My voice comes out breathy and weak.

His fingers slip under a band. "You first." He's bound to know that getting information out of an unfamiliar fae will be grueling.

"Being first is the best." I'm smiling, eyes half-lidded, until it sinks in that he has a hold of me. Shrugging, I step forward, testing to see how hard his grip is, but he lets go. I turn and bump into the cold stone wall. "I should just—"

"Go?" Do his eyes have the slightest reflection because they're so light, or because they actually glow?

"No." I point to the water. "I'm planning on bathing."

"Because of all the rolling." His frown tips back up again. "Good plan. Need company?"

"Definitely not." Even though he is a tempting treat, alone is best. I step into the edge of the pool, kneel, and scrub the panels of my silk skirt together.

"What's your name, tiny fae?"

I glare at his smirk. "What's yours?"

"You can call me Ty." He turns to run his thumb against the wall and I get a good look at his wings.

My fingers still, as does my body. However, my heartbeat quickens and my mind sprints.

His wings are thin gray membranes over narrow bones that look far more fragile than the rumors say they are.

He doesn't move from whatever he's examining. "You didn't realize, did you?"

CHAPTER SEVEN

YOU GO. NO, YOU GO.

TYPHON

I've come across Seelie before, and it rarely ends well. I don't see this being any different with the way her heart pounds as she eyes my wings, but this little hideaway was too great of a find not to take advantage of. That and the female hasn't a clue how to be stealthy, so I figured she wasn't exactly a danger. I could ask the ground to open and make a grand exit, but I can't seem to muster up the desire to do so.

She's beautiful. More so than any I've seen, and I am intrigued. The old scar along her cheek even adds to her unkempt beauty, though I'm not keen on the fresh bleeding scratches all over her.

"Unseelie," she whispers.

"Indeed." The tense silence sets my teeth on edge. "Let me guess. You've never met one of my kind, have you?"

She stands straighter and squints past me to the dim light coming from the cracks between the rocks at the entrance. "No."

I raise a palm toward her escape route. "Then run, little fae. I came here to relax, and you're interrupting. Go go; off to your flowers and family."

Her heart rate dials down a notch, and she inhales like she's going to say something, then blows out the breath instead. "I would, but...I need to relax as well, and since this is my territory—"

"Says who?"

Her angry huff is cute. "Says the Seelie High Court, who allowed the spring fae to place wards."

Is that dirt on her nose or a dash of freckles?

I bite my bottom lip. "Yet I'm not a Seelie, so your *Seelie territories* do not apply to me. Would you shoo a rabbit from your boundaries?"

Her gaze drops to my dick, which I appreciate. It's a great dick. "You're not a rabbit."

"No, I definitely am not. You're not leaving then?"

"No."

"Fine by me." I stalk toward the pond, but she holds up a hand. I feel like snatching it and dragging her to me, but then she really will think whatever rumors she's heard of my kind are true when so few of them are.

"You can't just stay." Her stance is proud and strong, much like highers in the Unseelie Court. It feels as if I'm under scrutiny at the main conference table, which is so very interesting.

Moving past her, I glide back into the warm water. There's a hot spring underneath that feeds and filters this pool. Not only am I not leaving, I'm revisiting this location as often as I can to escape my duties. I'm not even sure Donovan could find me, and my best friend—sometimes lover, oftentimes frustrating ball of wildness—is a master at worldwide hide and seek. I grin, wide and open. "Why not?"

"Because I need to bathe." Her proud face winces hard.

I settle back into my nook. "Then bathe."

The female whimpers in pain and doubles over. Before I can move to her, she shouts, "Because they'll find me if I leave!" Rubbing her temples, she gasps for air as if something had held her underwater.

I cluck my tongue. "The liar's curse packs a punch, doesn't it?" Serves her right. Still. I wave my hand and drag a few bunches of lavender I remember seeing outside through the earth until they pop up around the pond, turning the wet mineral scent floral. "Before who finds you?"

"Did you do this?" Her panicked eyes flit from flower to flower. Seelie really need to learn how to relax.

"Yes. It will help with the brain-slicing sensation. You should know better by now. How old are you?" I tilt my head. "Thirty?"

Her lips firm. "Seven. I'm thirty-seven."

I hum. "Now of Seelie breeding age." Then it all hits me. Trussed up, hiding, torn silks, and rolled in a field. I have a runaway bride on my hands. "You're hiding from the one who caught you. I assume you didn't enjoy the claiming?" I look over her soft curves. "Unfortunate."

CHAPTER EIGHT

AN UNFORGETTABLE OGLING

EMBER

My mouth opens, but fortunately nothing comes out because I shouldn't be talking to an Unseelie. They're dangerous, spiteful, quick to temper, mean to humans, and—now that I've met one in the flesh—incredibly tempting creatures from the dark side. How would I even explain my predicament to him without giving away too much about myself? Imagine if this Unseelie knew he was alone in a secluded cave with the only heir to the Spring Fae Court. The things he could do to hold the queen in his fist... not good. Nope. I need to survive the next few hours, escape being claimed, then press Mother about being an ambassador before she forces me to settle into the role she wants for me.

I undo my braids as I think of what to say, if anything. I shouldn't be around him at all. Yet I'm so curious. How did he even get here? Did he fly here with those dark wings, somehow skirting the magic wards we have in place? What do they feel like? He made lavender spring from the earth…to help me. Which it is. The searing pain is now a barely-there ache.

He shifts in the water, leaning forward, watching me so intently, my nipples tighten, and my wings grow hot against my back, my body clearly mixing up danger with potential pleasure.

I kneel in the water. "How does an Unseelie know about the Springfest Sprint?"

"The Springfest Sprint." That grin of his is dangerous. It makes things tighten inside me. "Isn't that an adorable name for something so disgusting?"

I scrub the silk panels together in the water. "As if Unseelie have nothing like it."

"We don't. Things like that are only created by Seelies and Selkies."

I wait for him to show any amount of pain, but he doesn't. "Then how do you choose a mate if you're undecided and come of age?"

He appears utterly confounded. "We wait until we find the right one for us."

Maybe they don't care about dwindling numbers.

I exhale a huffy laugh. "That must be nice."

"No. It's expected." He moves closer, dipping low in the deepest channel of the pond. "How's your new mate? Did he hurt you?"

The silk rips in my balled-up fingers, and I give up with a long sigh, falling back to land on my ass, warm water sloshing up to my chest. I cup my hands and splash my face. I'm enjoying the dark fae's attention and find I want to look decent in front of him—a good indicator of just how badly this day has gone. Moth dust rides the rippling water surrounding me in a patchwork that glitters in the dim light. "I vetoed. My only one. I couldn't fight him off."

He hums. "Hence the hiding spot."

I lay back in the water to work on getting the stick antlers from my hair, and the Unseelie—Ty—blows out a long breath. I look over to watch him watching me. My silks must be nearly see through in the water.

"So, you're not leaving?" he asks.

"No. Why?"

"You're distracting me. I am the opposite of relaxed."

I move backwards to the shallow edge of the pool and away from temptation, roll over and set my chin in my hand. "Can we be completely honest?"

"I think the liar's curse has us covered on that." He truly doesn't seem to care if I notice his eyes rove all over me, from messy hair to my backside emerging from the water to my crossed ankles in the air.

Even Jasper was polite about ogling. Then again, deep down on the inside, there's nothing polite about Jasper.

"What's it like being an Unseelie?" And why am I not afraid of him? Maybe it's the trauma I just endured or that I don't want to be part of this event. Maybe it's the curiosity and wanderlust my mother has chastised me for since my first wing flit. I've always wanted to travel but haven't been outside our court's mile without my community calling in a search party three flutters after I pass a border ward.

He smiles, bobbing closer. "You mean, what's it like being a murderous, evil creature of the night? Out for vengeance and reigning down chaos?" He makes a malicious laugh that booms around the cave.

Shushing, I splash him and glance at the exit as if the hunters would be waiting outside for the signal of an Unseelie's loud laugh. I turn back to glare at him. "You're going to get us found. But yes—what's it like?"

He wipes water drops from his face with his big hand, looking more amused than murderous. "I wouldn't know, little fae."

"Call me Em. Why not?"

He moves closer, water trailing as he reveals his big body little by little. He halts when the dark water just barely covers his hips, and I have to force my gaze away. "Because we're not murderous, evil, chaos creators. We can be vengeful, but with good reason—or better reason than your kind seems to harbor." He crawls closer through the water and mimics my stance, belly down, eye to eye with me. He reaches to nudge down the silk over my shoulder and loops a finger under a strap of the harness binding my wings. "This is a torture device meant to punish those who needed more time. That's vengeance. You should let me take it off." The soft purr in his voice does things to me it should not.

"I'm not allowed to until I'm claimed, or the race ends."

Chapter Nine

REALLY GOOD QUESTION

TYPHON

If the board finds out I was in a secret Seelie cave speaking to this gorgeous creature, upon my return, they'll string me up in the central square, so I'll be more accessible to the passersby. They all know how much I dislike the questions and how that would both punish me and delight my fans.

"What are you working on, Typhon?"

"When will we see the next invention, Typhon?"

"When are you taking the crown because your brother has been held hostage for moons by a coven of nymphs who have threatened to murder any Unseelie that crosses their borders, Typhon?"

I just needed a minute to myself, which is why it's so interesting that I don't mind this little fae's company. I'd like a lot more than just company, though.

The bindings she's wearing remind me too much of silken ropes and sex harnesses. I should be ashamed. She's wearing it for the psychotic claiming games the light fae conduct. And they call us evil. At least when we do a hunt, the participants are very willing and enjoy themselves immensely. I may have to host one when I return, though I doubt this fae would participate. If she were willing, I'd hunt her down, grip those bindings, and make a righteous mess of her. I'm so turned on that lying on the silken pond moss is painful.

And I'm zoning out as her pouty lips move, entrancing me along with the melodic timbre of her voice.

"What?" I ask.

Her eyes are a light orange and flash lighter, almost yellow, when she gets huffy. What color are they when she comes? "I said…" She brushes away my fingers from her hair, but not before I snag a dead leaf. "I can't take it off until I'm claimed, or the event is over. You didn't answer my question."

There was a question? "Fae are elusive like that."

"So you admit to being elusive?"

"Sure." I give her the expression that Donovan says gets him laid by proximity. "Just like you are."

Her left eyebrow raises in a slender arch. "Fair enough. Is your home dark and cold?"

I grin. "There is nothing dark and cold about my court. It's warm but very rainy. We have shelter structures built for sneak-storms. It's lit up at night."

"Lit up? How?" She glances back to her dimming light ball I propped on a vine, eyes beginning to glimmer again with what I assume is excitement. "Like that?"

"Bioluminescence." That's the more exciting one for most fae. "And electricity."

Her eyes widen and her lips part with a gasp.

I lean closer, unable to stop myself. "Are you impressed with me, tiny—Em?"

"Do you..." She looks around at the lavender. "*Make* the bioluminescence and—or—the electricity?"

Settling my fingers into the moss just a touch from the spill of her wet-silk-covered breasts, I pull what I need through the earth. After a minute of concentration, green glows from under my palm. I move my hand so she can see the tiny mushroom.

Her next gasp makes chills pepper my skin.

"No, I don't make it," I say, soft and low. "I pull it to me."

She touches the tiny fungus and giggles. "Can all dark fae do this?"

"No. And it's my turn for questions." I work the twig free from her tangled hair now that she's distracted by the glowing mushroom. "What is the claiming like in your event?"

She pulls her enchanting eyes up to mine as if to gauge my seriousness.

I tilt my head, trying to play coy because I'd like her to answer. "In theory, since you vetoed."

She looks back to the exit, then to me. "You get caught; you get claimed."

"How?" I need details. *Why?* I'm not entirely sure, but I feel the need to get this female talking about sex so I can see how she responds.

"We get fucked, Ty. Whichever way the hunters can manage it to prove we're theirs. Then we have a binding ceremony to lock the new couples together." The defiant glimmer in her eyes is sexy. "Though some don't fight like I did. Actually, one of the hunted was there to pick up my discarded veto. Most of the females were excited to have the chance with past flings or unrequited love interests. It takes the pressure off choosing." She goes back to poking at the dimming mushroom. "And then they're trapped forever."

"That's why you don't want to be claimed?"

Her relaxed position tightens up, and she backs away without answering, then steps toward the deeper water. She moves with fluid grace, and I wonder about her background, which is ridiculous because once she leaves this cave, I'll never see her again, so it doesn't exactly matter, does it?

Yet I turn toward her, noticing her eyes on my body, even when she's attempting to be discrete. I have to take the chance because an opportunity like this doesn't arrive every day. "How do you feel about fucking someone without being stuck with them forever?"

CHAPTER TEN

EMBER MY LOVE

EMBER

*H*ow do I feel about fucking? I laugh, unable to help it. "I love it when it's good, and it's still a decent day when it's not." At the deep side of the pond, the water reaches my chin. I dip under and comb through my messy hair, finally untangling the other stick.

When I emerge, Ty is close again, making my skin heat without him even touching me. "Have you thought about fucking an Unseelie?"

I lift my chin. "Of course I have, though I didn't picture them looking like you." I hold a hand up as he drifts closer. "I've also wondered what it would be like with those from other courts and other species of fae, humans, and elves. That doesn't mean I act on it."

I can't see well in such low lighting, but that makes his face—the shadows that bite over his straight nose, sharp cheekbones, and firm jaw—so perfect that I lose my breath. I shouldn't have stayed, but so far, he's been nothing but a gentleman. Far more than the males in the hunt, though that's expected of them, isn't it? Ty's earlier words come back to me. "*We wait until we find the right one for us. It's expected.*"

That's a bit of a mind twist, isn't it? So far, all I've been told about Unseelie is how dangerous and cruel they are. I've read the history of their demonic acts, though I suppose hexing unkind humans and wearing the blood of attackers never sounded that cruel to me. It seemed logical, though I kept that thought to myself. And the paintings made them look as if they came from the bowels of hell—face shadowed by evil, eyes of blood, body of sculpted death. I admit that Ty is dangerous to me, but I don't think it's because any of those rumors are true. His attitude isn't urging me to get away, and neither are his looks. I want to move closer to him and see how I fit against his bigger body. His bigger, *Unseelie* body. Understanding more about him and his people could become an obsession I carry for years. I've lost it. Jasper knocked the sense out of my brain with his tackle.

"Em," Ty coos, the inches between us disappearing.

Pebbles tink against boulders at the mouth of the cave, and we both turn to the sound.

"Are you in there, Ember, my love?" The question comes from far away, but also too close.

Dread floods into my bones. "Gentry Aspen," I whisper, air leaving my lungs.

"A gentry is after you?" Ty's eyes are wide and questioning.

I curse under my breath, moving to the edge of the pond as quickly but quietly as I can.

"Are you going to go to him?" he asks.

Any fae would chastise me for not wanting to become such a powerful position's plaything, so the question shouldn't annoy me, but it does. "No. He's a terrible kisser."

Ty chokes on a chuckle.

There is no escape except for the entrance Gentry Aspen is working his way through to get inside.

As we step out of the pond, I turn to Ty, lean close, and whisper. "I'm going to stand in that alcove"—I point to the itty-bitty cutout of stone next to the entrance—"and will hit him when he steps through."

Ty's brows snap together, and he looks at my hands. He doesn't realize I mean with a ball of light, or if Gentry Aspen continues…lightning. That's for the better. I'll be gone by the time Ty comprehends what I can do.

"The gentry will chase me, so just crouch in the corner on the opposite side, maybe. All will be as well as it can be." I stay close and inhale against Ty's collarbone. Goddess, he smells like earth and amber and my mouth waters. If I only had more time. "I'm glad I met you, Ty the Unseelie."

More rocks fall, and there's a grunt and a curse. "Why would she squeeze herself into this location, sir?" I gasp and touch my fingers to my lips to keep any more sounds out. Are they working together?

"And who is that?" Ty whispers against my ear. Even quiet, the tone he uses is more like I would expect from an Unseelie—a dangerous warning.

"Basil. He's the gentry's third." Why did I tell him that? I turn to run to my alcove as more pebbles and dry leaves fall, but Ty grips my wrist and pulls me back just as the gentry responds with an answer that I don't like one bit.

"Because Jasper said she went this direction. She's making this one hell of a game for me." He laughs. "She must know how much I enjoy hard-to-get females."

I move to sprint to the alcove before it's too late, but am snatched around the waist and hauled back into the corner where my light ball barely flickers. Ty tenses, and whatever is holding it sucks the orb into the wall, casting us in darkness.

"Ty," I whisper-yell. "I have to go."

"Not happening." He presses me against the wall and unfurls his wings before the cave shakes.

Chapter Eleven

R⊙TED CONVERSATION

TYPHON

The roots I call are thick and old, and I mentally apologize to the trees above for upending their quiet, solid existence. But the gentry and his third are not taking this female. She'll *hit* them? I almost laugh, but the thought is too sickening as I go through the likely outcome. She punches one; they both tackle her and do what I want to do... but with her being willing and enjoying herself more than any other time in her past. She loves fucking when it's *"good."* I can't even begin to break down that answer.

I huff and shake my head as the moving roots tickle over my wings, pressing us closer. And I'm naked. The wet silk of her—I guess it could be called a dress in a way—is cold against my skin, but I am very warm. I send a few roots over my clothing and bag that lie too far away for me to reach.

Ember gasps, and her hand lands on my chest, the other against my hip. I hold still, palms to the wall, pushing away to keep from crushing her. Her breathing goes erratic. I didn't stop to think that she may not do well in small spaces, especially in the dark, but it's this or dragging the males into the ground, starting a war with the spring fae, and scaring this little faery. I nuzzle the top of her head. This close, her fern and flower scent reminds me more of when the sun comes out after a rainstorm. I close my eyes at the relief of it and take a deep inhale. "Shh, sunshine. You're safe." The roots halt, and I relax, listening for the males, but they haven't arrived yet. Em—Ember—tenses further.

"It's so dark," she whispers.

"It will be dark for them, too. Do you all make light orbs?"

She shakes her head, tickling my lips, and her nails dig into my skin.

I refrain from telling her, "Harder." Barely. My cock thickens, and there's no way she doesn't feel me against her stomach.

She tilts her head up, orange eyes a deep sunset in the dark. "I can't even see you."

I want to lick her words, her tongue, her throat, and lower. "I can see you."

"Really?" she whispers, closing her eyes but keeping her head tilted up to me.

"Mm," I hum, moving a hand from the wall to graze her shoulder and trail my fingers up her neck. It's difficult with the cramped space, making my movements jerkier than intended, but she still tilts her head to give me better access.

"Ty," she says in a way that makes her intentions clear. *I need you. Please. Peel these cold silks off me and warm me up with your tongue.* But I want her to say it.

"Yes?" She does have freckles. I count them.

"Ember," a male voice singsongs. "Where are you?"

Losing count at thirty-two, I bristle, jaw clenching.

"It's dark as Morrigan's cunt in this place," the other male says. "Smells better, though."

I wince. The lavender. Too late to fix that.

"Language." That's the gentry, I think. "Start a flame."

"Fine, but she wouldn't come in here without lighting up the place. She's not here." There are stomps, a thunk, and a curse, then clicks of slate on slate further away. "Got it." The crackle of dry twigs comes closer, right, then moving left. "What's with the lavender—wait. She could have glamoured that."

Ember wrinkles her nose, and I run my thumb under her delicate chin. She could have?

"We would have felt that spell from anywhere in the territory," the gentry says. "I expected her to give herself away by now. Though I felt something earlier, but…" There's rustling. They're moving around the lavender stalks. "These are real, and look freshly planted. No one makes images like hers, but she can't construct plants like this. Probably."

I raise an eyebrow at her, not that she can see me. Being a master of glamour is a powerful gift. And a tangible glamour? Not possible. I think.

"Maybe someone's messing around with dim growing. It's not a bad idea. We could work on something over the summer and fall. It could help the food supply in the winter."

I don't hate the gentry. Winter growing is an honorable thing to work on. He really must have been a terrible kisser, but I can't say that's sad because I enjoy having his target pressed against me.

Ember's fingers tense again as steps approach. There's a tap close to my left. I don't dare move, but ache to pull my wings in tighter.

41

Chapter Twelve

LET'S NOT TALK

TYPHON

"Huh," the third says, stepping so close I can feel the heat of him against my wings. "Your new mate can work on low lighting training to develop the next seed generations."

The gentry is wandering, tapping on the opposite side of the cave, swishing through the lavender. "I like that idea. Just need to find her first. After that, I'm going to have to lock her up for a bit. No more playing hard to get. And I'll need to keep her away from Jasper. Veto or not, he's determined to bed her."

Ember has her eyes open again and is glaring hard.

How could anyone think this female would be happy being taken like this? I'm tempted to walk into the high court and demand an investigation into these types of events.

"She was good. Little bossy, but—I get to join sometimes, right?" There's pressure against my back. I think the third is holding onto a root.

Ember's face goes from fury to a raised eyebrow that makes me curious about her thoughts.

The push against me eases, and there's a flutter of wings crossing the room, easing the tightness in my muscles. All but my cock, which isn't relaxing at all, especially with Ember's occasional little shifts.

"No. Too risky in case she's fertile. You help, I'll make you second position, just like we agreed upon. No one but me touches her ever again."

Ember's eyes close, her nostrils flare, and she shakes her head.

I lean down, touching my cheek to hers so I can whisper in her ear. "That's not very fun, now, is it? Do you want more than one?"

She's quiet for a long moment, and her breathing picks back up. The slightest movement brings us closer, and a heated throb starts in my chest and spans out through all of me. She shifts the slightest bit, and her lips brush against my ear. "Why would I lock myself down to one when there are so many to explore? I'm not done yet." She would have made a better Unseelie.

"Let's try the Elkhorn," the gentry says.

"We could split up."

"And allow you to attempt claiming her on your own?" The pebbles fall again, and the voices grow quieter, thank the goddess. "Not a chance."

I believe we're both ready for them to be far away by the way Ember's tight stance slowly relaxes. Having a light fae more comfortable with me than her own kind makes my mind go places it shouldn't. I cannot steal the Seelie. That's not allowed. But I can protect her for now while having fun with her.

Sliding my fingers to the back of Ember's neck, I smile at the way her eyes flutter half-closed, and her lips part like she's experiencing this type of touch for the first time. "Another minute."

"I should go." She remains still, her chin tilted up to face me. "What if more find this cave?"

I'm not ready to let her go. "I'm going to block that entrance. Unless you'd like to glamour something."

"He wasn't kidding, Ty. It would call all the spring fae."

"You have power."

Her chest rises and falls, rubbing her tits and hard nipples against my stomach. "Can you shush and kiss me?" A fae with power that doesn't want others to know about it—that's a conundrum I was not expecting. Most fae brag, especially when what they say won't touch the liar's curse. "Or can you not find my lips in this darkness?"

I grin. Looks like there's no time for contemplation, because this impatient little fae has given me a request for a kiss, which I very much want to give. Hopefully, it will be far better than the gentry's. Tugging her closer, I tip her chin up by pressing a thumb to her jaw.

Her lips part in a gasp at the quick movement and I brush a kiss against her, feeling an unusual tingle. Is it because she's a Seelie?

I press in fully, fusing our mouths, closing my eyes as I savor the soft give of her lips and the way her scent infuses into my brain, setting my mind for one purpose.

Chapter Thirteen

NICKNAMES

EMBER

There is nothing mossy about this Unseelie's kiss. He tastes sweet and warm. Perfectly wet.

I tremble but from some energy trying to break out of me.

He stretches his hand until his thumb grips my chin, and he tugs my mouth open, giving a grumbly hum when I touch my tongue to his. With that greeting, we lose all caution we've both been exercising.

Pushing up on tiptoes, I press my aching chest to his body, and then get frustrated because he's too tall. I feel around in the dark, find his bare, incredibly firm shoulders, and start climbing. My knee presses against his soft wing.

He groans, cupping my backside. "Ember."

Him saying my name shouldn't tighten between my legs like it does, but apparently, my body is on board with this thing we shouldn't be doing. Our species steer as clear of each other as winter and summer. But it's impossible not to want him and discover if he can do other things as well as he kisses. Even if I get claimed after, I'll have this memory to hold on to for better or worse.

I pull my lips from his. "Is the coast clear? I need to see you." My whispers are frantic and tight. I should be embarrassed, but I can't seem to muster up that emotion in my desperation.

I think he's desperate, too, because he presses impatient kisses to my throat as he grinds his length against my thigh. We're in the most awkward position, clinging to each other in the cramped space he created to protect me—or maybe so we could do this. Either way, I'm beyond turned on.

There's movement behind him, startling me.

"It's just the roots." He brings his lips down to mine. For as desperate as he seems, his kisses remain teasingly gentle. He breathes heavily as I run my hands over him. He's warm marble; sleek and firm, but silky, too.

I feel around his thick torso, fingers finding the base of his wings. I gently explore the hard structure—bone and muscle wrapped in velvet.

He unfurls them, pushing the remaining roots away, then sets me down and turns away from me, looking around the empty cave that flickers in the firelight of the abandoned torch.

I step against his back, gripping his hips and kissing between his wings.

He gasps and exhales a groan. This close, I can feel the slightest pull of magic as he makes brush and roots fill in the gaps at the cave entrance. He turns to me, pushing me backward. His light eyes seem to glimmer with crimson, and if his cock wasn't a magnificently hard thing between us, I'd be afraid that he was angry. Especially as he jerks at my panels of silk.

I lean against the wall, touching my nipples as soon as he uncovers them.

As fabric hits the cave floor, he grips my wrists and stares at my chest with parted lips, then drops to his knees and laves each breast with his hot tongue. "Now touch yourself." The slickness makes my nipples more sensitive when I circle and tug them.

I moan, rolling my hips as he unwinds the makeshift, torn skirt.

When I'm free of everything but the bindings, he lifts my leg, draping it over his shoulder and pinning it there with his wing, and then... he licks between my legs.

I cry out, arching, but he doesn't let me move from the confusingly sensitive feeling.

He grins against me and licks again, then sucks. "You taste sweet, little fire."

I pant for breath and grip his hair, chills rising on my skin as tension builds between my legs. "A new nickname?" I ask between breaths.

"Trying them out, sweetness." He presses a finger against my entrance, then pauses. "Do you want me to fuck you, pet? Or is this enough for you?"

"More, Ty." Attempting to get his fingers inside me, I roll my hips and growl. "I irrationally need your cock. I'll explode if I don't feel you inside me."

"Thank fuck." He presses a finger inside me, pushing deep until I whimper at how good it feels. "So tight, love."

I like that nickname too much. "More. Faster." I bend to take his face in my hands and kiss him. I hope the person I end up tied to kisses as well as he does.

Another finger, and once he's stretched me enough, he speeds up his thrusts. "Like this, sweetheart?"

"Yes," I whine against his lips, wings thrashing against the bindings. "There!"

He graciously continues what's making my toes curl.

"Right th—" I cry out, pulsing violently around his fingers as he whispers how gorgeous I am when I come and how I'm soaking his fingers, and that's the sexiest thing.

His wing relaxes, releasing my leg, and he pumps slowly, patiently as my spasms subside, and I'm left with weak knees. Pulling his fingers from between my legs, he sucks them clean. This is by far the best sex I've ever had, and I think we're just warming up.

"Would you like to fuck my cock now, love?" His eyes are serious and maybe slightly concerned, but there's no sign of malcontent or that he wants anything other than a good time during a bad event.

I want that too. So much. As soon as I nod, he grips the lowest leather band of my bindings and jerks me to him.

"I'm going to go slow." He guides my legs around his hips. "At first. We'll see where it goes."

Chapter Fourteen

BINDINGS

TYPHON

Too brave and beyond sexy. I can see why hunters are seeking Ember, and I wish I had more time with her. If she were willing, I'd hunt her down, too, and I'm not even inside her yet.

She tastes sweet everywhere—lips, breasts, hip, and pussy. That makes no sense, but I may get an addiction to Seelie after her. That thought makes my stomach drop. *After Ember.* I clutch her to me, and she widens her legs around my hips and grabs my cock, making me groan in the best agony.

I'd thought her to be an impatient creature, but in this case, she swipes her thumb over the head of me to gather the leaking precum, slowly bringing it up to taste as she watches my eyes.

I nearly come.

She licks her lips. "Why do you taste so good, lover?"

My chest feels like it swells. "Trying on some nicknames of your own, sexy?"

"Maybe." She rocks against my length then angles her hips so the tip presses in, barely slipping into the heat of her.

I grip her bindings, wanting to rip them off, throw them, end this game, and steal her away from her court. But that's not allowed, nor would she want that. She's taking part in the event, and while she's hiding, that's her plan. Who am I to change that when I don't even know her? Unseelie also have traditions that others look down upon, but it's not their place to tell us we're wrong and steal our people.

Ember perches on the tip of my cock and I force myself not to slam up into her. Have her. Take her.

My heart explodes at her giggle, and I nip at her ear. "You're teasing me." I use her straps to drag her slowly down my length.

Her mood turns serious when I sink deeper into her tight, soaked heat.

"Doing well, pet?" I ask. She is so fucking tight.

She nods. "You're big. It's a lot but also really, really good."

I growl. "That word again...*good*. Let's see if we can do better than that." When I'm fully seated inside her, we stare at each other, still except for our panting breaths. As if we've been doing this for years, we move at the same time, tumbling into ravishing mouths, thrusting hips, touches that possess as we drag each other closer. Need rules us, and it is utterly delicious.

Her hips move against mine, working me with skill, and I growl against her lips, frustrated because I haven't even come yet, and I want more. That's not happening.

I have to remind myself of what this is to stay focused on getting a great fuck, and not how I need her in my bed for weeks, months. We could do good work there. "Do all Seelie fuck like this, sunshine?"

"Am I pleasing you?" she asks.

I pull back from kissing her neck to check her mood, and she gives herself away with a smirk. I tsk. "You're fucking me like a goddess, and you know it."

Her mouth drops open with a moan, and I quickly nip her lip. She giggles and turns her head. "Have you fucked many goddesses?"

I lean forward, lying her backward onto the ground, then grip her hips and pound into her. "Only one." I stare down at where I piston into this trussed-up beauty, who writhes and clutches at my thighs. "You're better." So much better. The best. I fit into her like a key to her lock, and there's a part of me that wishes she felt the same and would ask me to return. Maybe we can make this cave our meet-up adventure after she... the tightness in my jaw isn't from passion, and I'm not sure I've ever felt jealousy before. I crash against her harder, needier.

"Yes, Ty. I'm close. My goddess, you're so good with your cock."

I let go of her hip to slap it, grinning at her little gasp, and the shock in her eyes that quickly melts to lust. "I'm *great* with my cock, gorgeous. Play with your clit. You're going to scream for me and I'm going to paint those bindings with my cum so that anyone who gets near you will know I've been here."

She doesn't get a chance to touch herself as her back bows, and she keens a pretty note, tightening around me. She flutters inside as much as her wings do as they try to break free.

The tingle that's been weaving between us jolts through me, and I'm barely able to draw myself from her before painting her from her pussy to her breasts. My breaths come furiously, and I feel like I just spilled a lifetime of seed. I stare down at Ember and memorize every freckle, every aftershock moan, and the way her half-lidded eyes look back at me like this moment shouldn't end, even if it has to.

Chapter Fifteen

WHAT DO YOU WANT?

EMBER

Ty leans over me, encompassing my wings in his warmth, sliding in and out of me in a rhythm concocted to drive me out of my mind and somehow build me up to orgasm yet again. I hope the sprint is over because I'm not sure I'll be able to walk, much less run for several days.

His gentle caresses turn firm and needy. He's getting close. Gripping a strap of my bindings, he picks up his pace.

I arch my back, opening to him further, wanting him deep. "Can Unseelie get pregnant outside of a heat?" I ask. Our physiologies could mix some things up in our bodies if—

Gripping my hair, he turns my head and kisses me with a roughness that makes me purr. "No."

I suck his bottom lip. I want to keep part of him with me, even if it's temporary and there's no time or need to sort out my feelings about that. "Come inside me, please."

"Does that turn you on, pet?" He kisses a sensitive place on my neck, and his fingers blaze a path to my clit. "Or do you have ulterior motives?"

I grit my teeth and growl.

He slows, then completely stops his enthralling movements.

I shake my head and wiggle my ass against him, but he refuses to budge, even when I whimper a needy note.

"There's more to this," he says. "Tell me."

"Come inside me..." I sigh long. What does it matter anyway? "Come inside me and show the others who my pussy belongs to, even if I'm bonded to another." I drop my head between my arms, staring down at my fingers against the mossy ground. That's out there now.

His hand squeezes my breast to the point of delicious pain, almost feeling like he's digging in with claws, and he slowly starts his hips again. I guess I didn't scare him off mid-fuck, so that's something. He curls tighter over me and circles my clit with talented fingers. "I wish I had you in my bed right now, Ember. I'd fuck you to sleep and wake you by feasting on you for breakfast." His low-toned words make me gasp and roll my hips. "After that, I'd invite a friend over. He'd love these tits so much; he'd play with them for hours while I watched you squirm in frustration."

I make an obscene sound in my throat—like a choke and moan smashed together with a little disbelief and a whole lot of want.

The laugh that tickles my ear is dark and quiet. "You like that idea, don't you—two of us on you? Or maybe three? Do you think you could take three males, love, or maybe two and a female?"

I nod and whimper, unable to form words.

His thrusting turns as punishing as his words, because I won't get to try that. But I can picture it.

Heat floods my body as if I'm pulling it directly from Ty, and my body gives out as I tip over, crash, fall into maddening pleasure, chanting sounds that no Seelie has the right to make.

Ty holds me tighter and keeps pounding. His teeth graze my neck and gently bite into a sharp hold as he grunts and presses in so deep, lighting my core with his heat.

"Yes, Ty. Thank you," I whisper, breathing heavily. "Thank you." I never put myself in debt with thank yous, but he's earned it, maybe more than he knows.

He licks my neck and nods, pressing his sweaty forehead between my wings. "If things were different."

I swallow the knot in my throat and repeat his words, "If things were different," because that's the easiest thing to say about my feelings.

Not only is he not of my court, but he's also not of my kind. He doesn't know about my royal status and never will. He doesn't want me for more than this moment; I know it, and so does he. But it still hurts when he pulls from my body and kisses between my bound wings. And I damn near panic when he lies on the ground and drags me into his arms because I can't have this closeness ever again, and that realization hurts me more than I'd like him to know.

Pushing away from him, I plaster on a smile I wish I could glamour. I pull on dry silks, even though they're a rumpled disaster, and try hard to ignore the Unseelie's eyes on my every movement.

He stands when I turn to the door, and drags me into a crushing hug.

I cling to him painfully hard, and when he nudges his way to my lips, I kiss him with everything I have in me. It's his—I'm his. Just for this last, intense moment.

As soon as he sets me back on my feet, I turn and stride to the entrance of roots and brush. My heart beats in my throat as I wait in the silence, but I don't allow myself to turn around because I'll say something I can't say or do something I'm not allowed to do.

So I wait until roots shift, and I can move forward, navigating until I'm free of the cave, of Ty, and of the best experience of my existence.

CHAPTER SIXTEEN

DRAGGING IN THE FRIEND

TYPHON

I watch Ember leave with a tug in my chest that yells at me to follow her. But she doesn't want that, and I shouldn't either. She's a Seelie, and it's been hours—the best hours, yeah—but not enough time for her to show me who she is and have her judge me for who I am, or worse, want me only for what I am.

But I enjoyed being with her and am colder without her near me. That sass calls to me, as does the underlying vulnerability. And she didn't balk as I talked of multiple partners; she came hard.

I rub at my aching chest. There's a streak in her that's as dangerous as she must think I am, though I *am* dangerous. If I wanted to rip through her happy, flower-filled court to get to her, I could.

For the first time, I believe I'm experiencing what the original Unseelie felt that gained them their reputation.

I want what her kind isn't allowing me to have, and that's not quite fair, now is it? I could burn down this grove—drag spires of iron through it so that it would never be inhabited by fae again. No more Springfest Sprints, no more leaves the color of Ember's eyes or flowers that match her silks. I could take her and leave nothing behind but a trail of painful spring fae memories.

But that's not me.

Her kind would find a new home and hide away, telling nightmarish stories of the Unseelie who invaded during a sacred event. I doubt that would earn me Ember's favor. *Unfortunate.*

Dropping to my knees, I lick my lips, wishing I could taste more of her. It wasn't enough, but who am I kidding? A thousand moons might take the edge off, and yet, I'm doubtful.

I need help to work through this, but the only person who I want to talk it out with is far from here. Eh. He'll forgive me. I dress and touch my fingers against the moss, closing my eyes. The tug toward Ember still lingers in my chest, and for a moment, I worry, hoping I haven't just doomed my best friend to the core of the Earth because I'm distracted.

My concern only grows as the cave remains quiet. I'm about to dive into the earth to search when the water breaks.

Donovan surges from the pond, gasping. His dark curls are soaked and stuck to his face, and he looks around, squinting. "Ty? What in the name of Diana is happening? Why?"

"Shush. I have a problem."

He drops his head back and makes a rueful sound to the cave's ceiling. Is he bare?

I raise an eyebrow. "Did I interrupt?"

I get a faceful of pond water for that comment and grumble as I wipe it away.

"I should be growling, you insufferable cockblock!" He shakes droplets from his arms, walking from the water, and—yes, he is indeed bare-ass naked. "This better be so good."

I point at his jutting dick. "Anyone I know?" I have an inkling, and when his cheeks darken and he fans out his wings to dry instead of answering, I shake my head. "You two have got to stay away from each other." Anyone who doesn't know Donovan and Auralia are fucking thinks they're arch-nemeses. Their interactions are made of toxins and warnings.

His eyebrow raises. "Mm. Well, that's better said than done when she keeps cornering me and putting my prick in her mouth. You understand."

Maybe before today—she has a convincing tongue—but now, everything has gone a bit awry. "I have a problem."

Donovan looks over at me, and his brows furrow. "Oh?" He tilts his head and sniffs the air. "*Oh.* Did you just wander into this cave of sex, or is the scent of you and a female part of your problem?"

I exhale. "Last part."

That brings a smile to his lips. "Alright. Tell me all about it and I may forgive you for dragging me from my warm and occupied bed." He wanders around the cave, gathering leaves near the entrance. "Where are we?"

I inhale, still smelling Ember's scent in the air. "Spring fae territory." I tell him everything because he is my most trusted person and only sometimes steers me completely off the mark. By the time I'm done explaining—with only four gasp interruptions—he's fashioned himself a pair of shorts from leaves.

"So what's the plan?" Donovan asks. "My boxer-leaf-briefs and I are ready for anything. Except for a war, because that would not be a fun time."

I can't find it in me to quip back at him. "I need to get over this mini-infatuation. Which is why I pulled you here."

CHAPTER SEVENTEEN

NOT FAIR

EMBER

The forest is eerily quiet besides the hum of faery voices in the home tree's direction. Is it over?

I tiptoe between trees, but my body doesn't feel like my own. It's hard to move away from the cave because my legs aren't interested in heading any direction that doesn't include Ty. They'll get over it. He's probably gone by now, which is for the better. I don't need Gentry Aspen attacking him, then getting killed, then having to keep a war from happening between the light and dark fae.

I'm not sure what Ty's story is, though, or what status he holds. Maybe no one would come to his aid. Maybe the Unseelie wouldn't care if Seelie murdered him for trespassing.

Without permission, magic floods into me, slamming into the rage I was feeling, and I fight to hold on to it instead of releasing it, giving away my location. *What is happening?*

I cover my mouth with a palm to keep my heaving breaths from being too loud and lean back against an oak sapling, struggling to find comfort in the forest's scent and the quiet breeze. *Calm down, Ember.*

You're alone, and Ty is gone from here—safe. The magic calms as well, but it sits in my veins like it's on standby. I flex my fingers and rework my silk skirt panels when a sweet face peeks around a holly bush two trees away.

"Rain?" I whisper.

She lifts a finger to her lips.

"It's not over?" I mouth to her. It takes a couple of tries before her pretty eyes go sad, and she shakes her head.

I struggle again to hold in the magic that poured itself into me. I'm too far from the cave to go back, nor should I. If Ty were still there, I'm not sure I'd have the willpower to walk away from him, and where would that leave me? Heartbroken when he rejects me, or furious if he discovers who I am and takes advantage. Though isn't that what the male Seelie are doing today?

There's a crash through the trees, and Rain darts away, a mistake because Basil tackles her. She screeches a furious note and gives him a kick I wouldn't have expected from her.

I pick up a rock at the base of the tree I'm hiding against, but before I can throw it at him, there's another buzz of wings and Clay dives, slamming a knee into Basil's face, sending a burst of blood into the air along with a string of curses.

That's all the distraction I need, and I sprint toward the thorn grove as quietly as possible. My legs and my center are sore, reminding me of the last hours, as does the wetness dripping down my thighs. I may be slower because of Ty, but I don't regret that a bit.

Maybe if I can remain unbound, now that I'm of age, I'll ask around, travel, find him as an ambassador and get to know his bed and his friends for a few days. If he really was as kind as he seemed, there could be an alliance of some sort. My wings slam around, buzzing against the harness that was loosened by Ty's grip. When I visit, maybe I'll bring it with me for old times' sake and let him take it off me like he wanted to. I shake my head at my foolishness.

Mother was right; daydreams are for children and non-royalty. It may not be fair, however, I have duties to my people—responsibilities that would make things fall apart in my absence.

But the gravity of this stupid tradition is all too real when Gentry Aspen drops to the ground in my path.

Chapter Eighteen

QUICK AS A SNAKE

EMBER

"I like how we play, Ember." Gentry Aspen clasps his hands behind his back, looking at me from my dirt-stained toes to my disastrous hair. His gaze returns to my neck and I'm positive Ty left marks there. The gentry takes a step toward me, appearing confused when I take one back. "The game is over now. I've got you."

"Is that what you think?" I ask, gathering the surging magic into my center.

He raises an eyebrow. "Still playing then?"

I shake my head. "No. I just don't want you for a mate. I don't want..." I swallow down the thick words that refuse to budge past my lips because it would be a lie. There is someone I want, even if it's ridiculous to do so.

His gaze hardens. "Don't want what? I can give you anything."

My laugh is sarcastic and probably cruel, but I'm unable to care. "No, you can't."

"Look, Ember." Another quick step forward from him has me scrambling back. He glares. "This is the way things are, and I've chosen."

"Did you ever stop to think that I've chosen? I didn't leave you that night to tempt you into chasing me—I've told you that, but you refuse to listen. I didn't like how you kissed, and I won't live with that forever."

Looking shocked, he licks his bottom lip, then goes back to scowling. "There's no need for kissing." The step he takes forward isn't hesitant.

"If you don't need to kiss, then you're doing it wrong," I yell, letting the magic snap into shape. He wants a chase? It's on.

Twenty brown snake glamours slither off in every direction, all exact replicas of the glamour suit I'm wearing.

He curses and launches off the ground, a terrified grimace on his face.

I have to bite my lips together to keep from laughing. Snakes don't laugh.

Unfortunately, they're not hearty either, and to my right, he flies through the closest one to him, arms out, I assume to catch me. When that one dissipates, he's already on the next. That won't take him long.

I breathe in, and the magic still simmers inside me, full and ready. It's odd, but I'm not going to question it because I need it now. I duck under a bush and pause, hoping he's too distracted by the chaos of scales that he doesn't notice one snake halted. My next trick takes concentration, if it works at all. I lull my head, loosening the tight muscles of my neck and taking big breaths. Gritting my teeth, I spin my next glamour, swirling the forest.

There are screams in five different directions, and I keep my eyes closed, mentally apologizing to the others who are not interested in owning me but also simultaneously patting myself on the back for my good work.

I got the idea for this glamour after getting stuck in a dust devil. When it slowed enough to spit me out, I was so dizzy, I couldn't stand up for too many flutters, and even then, it took several more to function correctly. I drop the glamour as fast as I created it, hearing more screams and several thunks of faeries to the ground. Then I open my eyes and I'm back to running, though instructing my snake glamour to slither.

I watch the air, listening for wings and yelling as I run toward the thorn grove. It's further than I'd like and the hunters are bound to have recovered by now, but maybe my whirly move is keeping them grounded longer. I can only hope. When I drag myself up the hill to a small hole I know I can fit through, I halt in disbelief.

The thorns are gone. Someone has shaved the stems from the ground to a full inch above my head. This was so much work.

I just blink until I hear a buzz of wings, then I haul myself through the not-at-all-dangerous entrance. Maybe I'll get lucky, and any following hunter will get tangled and stuck. I pull a face. Not likely.

CHAPTER NINETEEN

PARTING WAYS

EMBER

"Ember!" At least Gentry Aspen isn't using that damnable song this time when he bellows my name.

I leap over winding, woody stems, heart pounding as the inevitable bears down on me, so close I can hear his breathing and prepare myself to be tackled. A twisted stem makes the perfect foothold and I leap to it, then climb up to the thorny growth, only nicking my wrist once. There's no point in holding the glamour, so I let it go.

"Get down here this instant." Gentry Aspen paces below, wings flitting against the thornless stalks.

Once I catch my breath and can manage words, I yell back. "No. Obviously."

"Stubborn female." He grips the stalk I'm attached to and shakes it, sending me swaying into the surrounding stems.

I shriek when a thorn stabs my shoulder. "Stop before you nick my wings."

"That would be on you, Ember. Climb down, or it's going to get worse." He puts his hands on the stalk again and then gasps as the ground beneath him crumbles, sucking him down. He struggles and claws at the surrounding vines, looking up at me in disbelief. "What is this?"

My stem sways sideways again, and I hold on tight, bracing myself for the impact against more thorns, but it never comes. Nor do I move back into place. I just freeze, arched over my stem that has paused in the air.

Gentry Aspen yells, "Unseelie!"

I lift my head fully, nearly falling.

Sprigs of thorns bend, creating a V-shaped channel, and in the midst of open space is Ty and another Unseelie, large gray wings flapping to keep them hovering. They're silent. Ty slowly moves forward, clothed in black pants and a long crimson vest with a wild embroidered design in black. His boots appear to be a type of velvet. So fashionable.

A wave of relieved heat and tingles swirl through me, feeling like it's mixing with the magic that just won't vacate my body.

"Do not touch her, demon," Gentry Aspen yells, spitting and struggling as he spews threats.

The other Unseelie's laughter is melodic and deep. "If he only knew." His smile is big and bright. He doesn't have the eye for fashion that Ty does, but I appreciate his state of near-undress because he's gorgeous, too, with an array of mounded muscle, though he looks nothing like Ty—he's darker with softer features.

Ty glares down at Gentry Aspen, then back at me, eyes touching over my skin, raising chills when he sidles up next to me. "Hello, sunshine." His lips cast down as he wipes at the blood on my shoulder with his sleeve. "Would you like me to send him to the core of the Earth?" He appears quite serious.

The rant from below halts for a moment before restarting. "Ember? Who is this fiend? How do you know him?"

I ignore the gentry and keep my eyes on Ty.

He's breathtaking in the late daylight, and his lips quirk in a way that makes me want to kiss him again.

"No," I say. "Don't let him out for a bit, though. Apparently, the game is still going."

Ty's jaw clenches. "I suppose I should be thankful for that, in an unlikely way. You're not claimed."

"Not caught yet. The assistance is appreciated." I look over his handiwork. "So you can bend branches, too?"

Ty tips his head toward the other Unseelie. "That would be Donovan's doing. Say 'hello' Donovan."

"Greetings, lovely." The charmer winks. "Thrilled to meet the reason my best friend is putting our lives in jeopardy. Though I'm kind of getting it." He scans my face and disheveled outfit as I cling to my stem. "Can we, like, hurry?" He checks behind him and shakes his head. "Well, Ty, you wanted witnesses."

"Witnesses?" I look in the direction that's caught Donovan's attention. The spring fae army is on the move, navigating the forest like a flock of migrating birds. I glare down at Gentry Aspen. "For the love of crepes, did you call the entire legion?"

He tries to dig his way from the ground that's swallowed him to his waist. "They're Unseelie, Ember. Here to wage war."

"They are not." I look back at Ty. "Right?"

He shrugs a shoulder. "I suppose that depends on the next couple of minutes."

CHAPTER TWENTY

UNEXPECTED MATCH

TYPHON

Do I want to immobilize a court army? Not really. Will I to prove that I can? Oh, absolutely.

I hold my hand out to Ember, trying to stay patient when, really, I'm a mess to get her back into my arms. If that thorn prick had been against her wings, she could have fallen. I wouldn't put it past these wretched faeries to continue their game, even if she'd broken a leg or been unconscious. Then they really would join the Earth's core along with the rest of the spring fae for allowing this event to happen.

I focus with a deep breath, and a long stare into her eyes, struggling to find my patience. "Would you like to get away from the thorns?"

"Yes." She reaches for me, arms wrapping around my neck, legs around my waist as if she knows I'll do anything to keep her safe.

I palm her ass and stroke her cheek with my thumb. We both lean in for a kiss. There's an unsettling jolt in my chest, distracting me from her perfectly soft lips. It's not that the kiss is bad—it's so good to have her against me—it's just that it's a teasing taste of something I need desperately. I want all of her, but there are rules for both of us. If she wants me.

"Stop that!" the male below yells. "How dare you kiss her, you—"

Ember settles closer, her breasts pressing against me. A pretty flush lights her face; something I couldn't see well enough in the dark cave.

I want to tug her silks aside, rip off her bindings, and hold her bare against me. There's a part of her that needs me, and I enjoy it so much, it hurts to think of not having her near me ever again. That's why I needed Donovan—to convince me not to do this or to come along for the ride. And here he is.

"Go south," Ember says, gripping my shirt. "There's a point where you—or maybe we—can escape, and there are no flying fae past that border."

"Good thinking." I lift us further in the air, heading toward the incoming army with Donovan beside me.

"Ty?" Ember clings to me, body going stiff. "What are you doing?"

Donovan snorts a laugh. "She really doesn't know, does she?"

"Know what?" Ember's voice is laced with panic. "Ty?"

"I know it's confusing, love. Just hang on." I wrap my arms more tightly around her and dive to land, setting her on her feet and taking a painful step away from her.

The Seelie yell orders as they surround us, pointing spears and holding shields.

Ember stands in front of me with a demanding presence. "Don't."

A male in hunter's garb runs toward her.

A sharp snap of magic breaks the air as Ember sends a ball of crackling electricity at the male.

He cries out when it makes contact, sending him sailing back and rolling along the ground, bumping into those who couldn't move in time.

The rest of the crowd goes quiet and takes a collective step back.

"Ohhh," Donovan says, beside me. "Okay, yeah, I really get it now."

I shake my head, keeping my eyes on Ember. "I didn't know she could do that. You throw lightning balls too?"

Ember nods, looking sheepish instead of proud. Odd.

"What is the meaning of this?" The female who steps forward must be the queen. She's regal and dainty. After snapping her fingers at a group of guards, sending them off toward the thorns, she lifts a proud chin. It reminds me of Ember's defiant gaze.

I bow, as does Donovan. "We mean no harm," I say, then continue before I get speared by one of the many angry guards. "However, I'd like to extend a request."

"What's the request?" The queen wears a sharp frown.

Donovan nudges me and whispers, "You sure because..." He raises his eyebrows, eyeing the large, shifting crowd.

"You're my witness in case there's a dispute from our court," I whisper back. "And my second if the Seelie try to chop our heads off." Taking a deep breath, I turn to Ember and hope this doesn't get me killed. "I, Prince Typhon Redrek Jenderos of the Unseelie Crown Court, would like to present a formal request of pursuit to Ember." My pledge using my full name is enough for tingles of magic to sizzle over my skin.

Both the queen's and Ember's jaws go slack.

"Oh," Ember whispers.

"What does that mean?" a male says, eyeing Ember with heat in his eyes.

"It means..." the queen interrupts before I can move to rip the asshole's head off. She holds up a finger as two fae in royal garb whisper in her ear. "It means that there's a proposal from a royal Unseelie in the middle of the Springfest Sprint. And what do you say, Daughter?"

"Daughter?" I tilt my head, looking Ember over with fresh eyes.

Donovan barks a laugh that makes the crowd jump in sync. He holds his hands out. "Don't attack; I mean no disrespect. It's just... they didn't know they were both royals."

The crowd falls into murmurs of chatter as Ember and I blink at each other. The princess of Spring Seelie and the prince of Crown Unseelie.

Ember makes a dainty snort and smiles, turning to her mother—the damned queen—and raising an eyebrow. "You'll allow it?"

I honestly didn't think about a potential rejection from the queen, as the Unseelie courts have been throwing their offspring at me for a decade in hopes one would stick.

The queen tilts her head. "I will need to speak with the Unseelie crown king."

"He is, uh..." Donovan wrinkles his nose, then smiles. "Detained by nymphs."

The queen narrows her eyes and lifts her chin. "Where?"

"The Rioch Coven in the midlands."

The crowd breaks into murmurs, and I nod to confirm. "We're unsure when they will release him. If they release him. We're in conversations." Which are going nowhere, but they are happening. I really need Kage back in the castle, especially if I'm bringing home a Seelie bride.

An older male holding a flagon and swaying on his feet lifts a finger in the air. "Will they take an exchange?" he slurs.

The crowd finds that funny, though most still keep a wary eye on us.

I take Ember's hand.

Like a magnet, she slides against my side. She peeks at her mother, who is busy listening to the whispers of her posse.

The queen's lips tilt up, and she flicks her fingers at Ember, like she's asking her to get on with it.

Ember looks up at me, eyes sparkling yellow. "I, Princess Ember Firelight Morinaktune, accept your pursuit and wish you well."

My heart about bursts out of my chest.

Until the queen says, "But just as the Unseelie have traditions such as courtship rules, so do Seelie. We're in the middle of a competition of claiming rights. Your pursuit will not interfere with the games." Her smile is dreadfully wicked.

Chapter Twenty-One

WELL, THEN, FINE.

EMBER

He's a freaking prince. I could laugh. Except I'm still in the Springfest Sprint, and four competing males surround me.

Basil has recovered from my lightning strike and grins, shifting from foot to foot. Half his face is a bruise and one eye is swollen shut. Good work, Clay.

Jasper glowers with Storm smiling smugly behind him. I assume they're now together, no matter how sour he appears.

The other two are Stone, who I'm assuming didn't get to Quartz in time because he's seething, and Leaf, who seems to care about this event as much as I do. His arms are crossed and there's not a red hair out of place as he eyes Donovan with heat. I think Leaf may be my new best friend.

I turn to Mother, not releasing Ty's hand, though I'm not sure he'd let me. "Are the same rules in place for Ty—Prince Typhon?"

Mother listens to her advisors again, then nods. "Fights to the death are not allowed. There will be no freeing the bound wings of a female until a claiming has occurred, and an official referee must be present in order for the claim to be valid." She points to Ty, and Willow steps from the crowd to flutter next to Donovan, though she keeps her distance, eyeing him warily.

Ty leans down to whisper in my ear. "It's unfortunate that we didn't have the witness earlier. Now we have quite the crowd." His gaze is a challenge.

I blink up at him. "Do you think I'm going to make this easy on you, Prince?" While it may be a simple solution to push aside my skirts and jump on his cock, I'm not doing that in front of the entire spring fae community. They'll make fun of me for eternity, look down upon the princess who gave it up with no fight to an Unseelie prince, and I kind of want him to chase me.

Donovan blows out a breath. "Can I join?"

"Another day," Ty growls, keeping his piercing gray eyes on me. "Let's get started then, my love." He's beautiful in both shadow and light.

I about melt into the ground and bite my lip to keep myself from biting his.

Donovan clears his throat and raises his voice so all can hear. "By Unseelie tradition, the official pursuit comprises the request, the wooing, the gifting, a physical exchange—" He flicks Ty's forearm, and Ty reluctantly lets my fingers go. "In order, you animals," Donovan whispers, waggling his eyebrows and making me giggle. He straightens again. "Then there's an exchange of intentions, then acceptance or denial."

Mother nods along with me, even though her advisors surround her, arguing and whispering. Looks like we agree for once. What a surprise.

Ty smiles down at me. "Ready?"

There's a buzz of wings, and the guards arrive with a murder-ous-looking Gentry Aspen.

Mother looks smug. She still thinks he'll win me.

I step closer to Ty but don't touch him. "I *am* ready. You may want to close your eyes."

I do the same and let the magic swell inside me—though it feels oddly endless—then set the world spinning again as I quickly tip-toe past the screaming crowd, eyes squinted and focused on my feet. Bringing the glamour to an abrupt halt, I sprint away, ignoring the curses and sounds of retching. There are not a lot of hiding options since the thorn grove and cave were discovered, but maybe I'll find luck in the goldenrod field. It's not far, and I dive between poofy yellow plants, taking on the yellow pigment as I run. Once I'm sufficiently covered, I slow and sneak deeper into the field, taking care not to disturb a stalk and give away my location. I turn toward the buzz of wings and back into a hard body. With a yip, I swing around.

Ty grips both my wrists. "Now the nickname 'sunshine' really does fit. You're bright yellow."

"If this is your version of wooing, you have to do better."

His lips tip up. "How about if I tell you I'm entranced by how your pussy felt fluttering around my cock and I want that daily for the rest of my life?"

"Demanding," I purr.

He tugs me closer. "You have no idea." He leans in, setting my whole body into flames of lust, and whispers in my ear, "And I love how you smell like the first sunbeams after it rains. I want you to see our city and rainstorms; meet our people at shows and dinners." His words send tingles down my neck.

"You mean that." Of course he does. The liar's curse would punish him if he didn't. "And you want me in your bed?"

"Our bed, yes. Are you wooed yet because—" He points up to an incoming hunter.

I jerk from his grip and dart into the field.

Ty growls behind me.

Donovan laughs. "You chose a spicy little thing, Ty."

"Don't call me little," I yell, then squeal as Basil darts into my path. I throw a light ball at him, and thankfully the sparks I smacked him with earlier are still fresh in his memory because he yells and crashes sideways, shielding himself.

A buzz to my right is so fast I drop to the ground and front roll, barely evading Gentry Aspen's grip.

"I asked you a question, sweetheart," Ty calls from the sky, voice hard. "Are you wooed enough?"

He sounds like that's important, but I'm busy dodging.

Gentry Aspen swoops my waist and I glamour a redcap goblin lifting a hammer beside him. He screams and lets me go, but my trick only works a second before he tackles me to the ground.

CHAPTER TWENTY-TWO

THOROUGHLY WOOED

TYPHON

Ripping the gentry into two irritating pieces is more tempting by the second.

Donovan knows it and puts his hand on my shoulder. "This is more difficult than I thought it would be, but she has to choose you."

For my traditions, she does. "I know, and I fucking hate that right now."

Our referee has been keeping her distance, but drifts closer, ear cocked towards us to hear our discussion.

"You can ask us anything," I tell her, annoyed.

She licks her lips. "Why would you hate that she has to choose you?"

I keep my eyes on Ember. "I could take her in a second if it were only her traditions to worry about. But my people may contest me for taking Ember as my bride, saying I yielded to her Seelie rules instead of our Unseelie traditions. They could claim the binding invalid."

Donovan sighs. "And you couldn't have waited to pursue her. She wouldn't be available per her traditions because they're not going to let her get away."

I grit my teeth as Ember escapes the gentry's grip, just to be caught again. "This situation sucks a toad's rump."

Donovan snorts. "Yep."

Lifting my eyes for a second, I glance at the referee, and signal below. "We're not the monsters you consider us to be. We'd never let this happen."

My soul jolts at Ember's screech. I'm about to forgo protocol when she yells. "I'm wooed. Gods to all, I am so wooed by you, Typhon."

Donovan releases my shoulder. "Don't rip his head off."

"What if it's accidental?" I ask, tucking my wings and swooping down.

"I have to advise against it," the referee says.

I grip the gentry's waist, and when he lets go of Ember to fight me, I spin and throw, launching him away.

Ember tugs her ripped silk somewhat back into place, though her right nipple peeks at me as she shifts. "We have to do this at the same time, don't we?" When I nod, she puts her hands on her hips. "I've been asked and wooed. Next—" She holds a hand out.

"Impatient?"

She narrows her eyes, and I'm tackled to the ground.

The fae that punches me in the jaw shouldn't be as strong as he is, and stars blink in my vision for a moment.

When a sharp pull of magic shifts in the air again, I dodge as his fist dents the ground. I shove myself up with my wings, flinging him away from me, then drag roots up to capture his ankles and waist.

He screams a hoarse cry, reaching for me with grabbing fingers. "Free me. Free me!"

I nearly feel bad until I realize Ember has disappeared. No, this assberry can stay trapped.

Two sets of wings buzz, circling over the field.

I look at Donovan and the ref, but they remain quiet. Closing my eyes, I touch my chest. There's something there now that's full and attentive—has been since I saw the delicate way Ember stepped into the cave and then attacked me with light. A tug.

My lips quirk and I extend my wings, taking to the air and flying toward where my intuition tells me to go.

The gentry notices first and bares his teeth at me.

The temptation to show him my fangs is too much, and I let that darker version of me slip out, the one I'm not sure Ember will appreciate.

She didn't notice in the dim cave with me behind her or seem to realize the graze of my fangs as I held her in place while she came apart beneath me. I'd lost control around her—understandable—but forced myself to hold back, though the inner fire inside me wanted to roar alive and consume everything.

"Ty," Donovan warns, then curses as I surge forward.

There's no stopping me because I can feel her, and he—the one who wants to take her from me—is too close.

The gentry and I meet mid-air in a crunch. I get a knee to the stomach but clock him hard on his temple.

He's big for a Seelie. Not my size, but close. He shakes off my punch and comes at me again.

When Ember screams, I dive without thought, leaving the gentry flailing.

When he catches up to me, I kick out hard, sending him sideways.

There's a sharp magic snap, and the third—Basil—tumbles through the air towards me.

I grip the tiny cloth covering his crotch and rip it from him as he spins by.

Ember stands on the ground, more disheveled and looking mad as a wolverine. That changes when she takes me in, and I worry she'll fear me now.

Landing in front of her, I extend the cloth. "A gift to commemorate this occasion."

I can practically feel everywhere her gaze touches: the shadowed tint making my features more prominent, the crimson I'm sure touches my irises, and the tips of my fangs—longer than they've ever been.

She swallows hard. "You look dangerous, Unseelie."

Chapter Twenty-Three

I THOUGHT...

EMBER

Dark shadows paint Ty's pale skin in the hollows of his cheeks, collarbones, and around his eyes, which now gleam red. He looks like a vengeful god, and I both fear and want him.

What does it say about me that between my legs is tight and pulsing, and that the odd magic that's been swirling inside me wants to be released?

Before I can consider my concerns, Gentry Aspen flies towards us with murder in his eyes.

I throw lightning at him, and don't feel a bit of guilt as the peephole cries out and tumbles to the ground. That may have been too much but I'm tiring of this game and of these males chasing me like I'm a rabbit to be taken down for their needs alone. Ty never made me feel that way. Not once.

He stares at me with concern and acceptance, as if waiting for me to throw lightning at him, too.

I snatch the fabric from his newly-formed claws and leap on him, planting a kiss on his slack lips. "I accept this gift." Then I drop from him and run, trusting him to follow.

His wings are oddly silent in the sunset, and with the light growing dim, I bet he can hunt me even better. I doubt he'll stray from me again, but I can't hear anything except my pounding feet and quick breaths. He's drawing this out, letting me think I can get away as I dart through bushes and spin around trees. Right? He has to be. Unless he changed his mind.

The buzz of wings behind me makes me slide behind an oak and peek, but it's only Willow, staying close.

Donovan isn't around, nor is Ty, and my heart races. Maybe there was trouble? Did the other three gang up on them? I can't wait around to find out; I need to hide.

My wobbly legs protest as I run toward a hollow tree. I dive for it when an arm scoops my waist, and a big hand grips my throat. I panic and kick out, but the angle I'm held at prevents me from landing anything.

"Caught you, hellion," Ty grumbles against my ear, then sinks the fangs I caught a glimpse of earlier into the spot just above my collarbone.

I cry out at the sting, but then heat pulses through me like venom. Oh, whoa. Do I like this? I think I do.

He jerks my silks aside, tugs at his pants, then pushes me face-first against the tree. Releasing my shoulder, he licks my skin and surrounds me with the heat of his bare chest. "Sweetness. Would you like me to claim you now?"

I press my palms against rough bark. "You have to ask me that?"

He slaps my bare ass hard, making me yip. "Yes, I do. Do you accept?"

Reaching back, I squeeze his hip. "I do."

He kicks my legs apart, then lines up and slams into me with one hard thrust, then stays still, buried deep inside me. "Claimed, my love." He jerks hard at the bindings around my torso, snapping them with his claws as he frees my wings. He drops a kiss between them as they unfurl.

I hiss at the sharp ache.

Ty gently caresses the cramping away. "Beautiful."

My wings flutter with his compliment before he pulls from me, turns me around, lifts me, and crushes me against the tree, pinning my hands above my head and giving a gentle peck to my lips before he grips my thigh and slams back inside me with a grunt.

He fucks me like he can't get deep enough, fast enough to sate his furious passion, and all I can do is hold on—hold on and notice that over his shoulder, Donovan and Willow watch on.

Willow nods like she understands this was the best outcome for me, though her expression isn't pleased.

Holding Ty's vest, Donovan watches us like he's ready to join, and I wonder if he's the friend that Ty mentioned in the cave when we were talking about the things we wished we could have. We can have that now.

I lick my upper lip and moan as Ty thrusts away.

Donovan grins and is definitely outgrowing his odd leaf shorts. Yeah, it's him.

There are other watchers too. Gentry Aspen's singed face is harsh with fury, and he flies off, but Basil stays to watch us, uncaring that he's fully naked and aroused.

I find I don't mind it and struggle until Ty releases my wrists. Sinking my fingers into his hair, I kiss his panting lips.

His tongue tangles with mine, and I groan.

When we part, I drop my head back against the tree and grin at him. "I want to kiss you every day."

"I want that too." Ty tips his forehead against mine. "I will treat you with respect, Ember. And care for your needs with everything I am."

This must be the intentions part of his traditions.

I re-shift my legs around his hips. "I accept that and will do everything I can to keep you happy and safe." Leaning close to his ear, I whisper, "That means fucking often and setting our enemies on fire with lightning, lover."

He thrusts so hard that my teeth clack together, then rumbles a laugh when my core tightens. "Come for me, Ember."

"No need to get bossy." I moan and arch back, letting him grind me into an orgasm that makes me scream out and claw at his back.

Gritting his teeth, he thumbs my bottom lip. "You'll find out how bossy I can be sometimes, sunshine."

I grin with loopiness, and the magic that's been building loosens and swirls. I can't hold it and don't want to. "Ty," I chant, as it gains a momentum inside that's both terrifying and right. "Ask me."

He grins, though it looks pained as he rides that precipice of pleasure. "Do you accept my pursuit?"

"Yes!" I shout as my pussy pulses again and the magic settles into my soul like it has found its new home.

Ty pumps twice more and roars his release, sending me into deeper pleasure until exhaustion drags me under.

Chapter Twenty-Four

THE AFTERMATH

TYPHON

Ember goes slack in my arms.

I'm not far behind her. I turn and slide down the tree, curling my wings around us and sighing as I settle between the roots.

"Congratulations," Donovan says, stepping forward. "This is not how I expected my day to go."

"Nor did I." I grin, too giddy, as I look down at my beautiful little bride.

More Seelie approach, bringing chatter with them, as well as flowers. They set petals around us, still seeming wary but accepting the bond, which is good because Ember and I are very bonded—no mystical mate walk or binding ceremony needed.

Her blood was the finest wine on my tongue, and I realize now why every taste of her was so sweet. She'd been seeping into me from the moment we touched, just as I had her, and when she accepted me, I felt the essence she'd already marked inside me settle, lighting up the darkest stretches of my soul.

My True Mate.

I'm not sure what it all means yet, but we will have all the time to figure it out together.

The surrounding fae laugh and murmur. "The binding is strong. Do you feel it?"

"Everyone feels it. Maybe his people do too."

Maybe they're right.

Donovan talks quietly to Willow, and a mateless redheaded hunter slinks in to introduce himself.

Others find their way to my friend with caution and questions. Fortunately, everyone leaves me and Ember be.

I trace her freckles, then tuck her messy hair behind her pretty pointed ear.

She inhales against my chest, and blinks open her eyes. They match the bright yellow specks of pollen still clinging to her skin.

I hug her to me more tightly with my wings. "Are you okay, tiny fae?"

She pinches my nipple. "Don't call me tiny."

Chuckling, I grin down at her. "Oh, good. You're just fine."

Turning her face, she kisses my chest. "Better than fine. You?"

"Yes, but I'll be even better when there's not a crowd of faeries surrounding us while my cock is still inside you."

"Oh, yes, I can imagine how that may be slightly uncomfortable." She tenses her pussy.

I inhale sharply and glare down at her. "Be good or I'll stretch my wings and show off my handprint on your backside."

She bites her grinning lips together but doesn't tease me further. "Do you think we were rash, Ty?"

I shake my head. "If we hadn't been, we wouldn't be bonded."

"Good point. I wouldn't want that."

"I'm glad. I won't be like the gentry—what he said. That's not—you can do as you wish, love."

Ember smiles and leans in closer. "I'm going to want you a lot. I think I'm going to be very demanding of you, Typhon."

"Good, my little sunbeam. Because I'm looking forward to learning everything about you." I nip her chin. "Including each fantasy you've thought about in detail. How to tease every type of moan out of you."

The growing crowd parts, and the queen steps through, taking us in with a sharp glare. "Where is Gentry Aspen?"

Ember sits up, making me wince because having a conversation is going to be difficult when I really want to fuck her more, and since I'm already in her...

"Why do you care so much, Mother?" Ember glares back, chin raised.

"Because he's the strongest of us. He should have—"

"He's not the strongest of you," I interrupt. "Ember is." I carefully slide her from me—though it pains me to do so—tug my pants up and stand, setting her on her feet and wrapping a wing around her since she's only covered by one ripped silken panel. "And now she's bonded to me. That will never change."

"Is that so?" The queen smiles in challenge.

I bristle hard.

"That *is* so," Ember says. "Can you not feel it? Typhon is mine, and I am his. We're bonded forever and if you'd like my help to run this court, then you will do nothing to interfere with that. As of now, I am free to do what I want, and will travel to his court to see his electricity and rain and to meet our people." She turns to me. "Right?"

The crowd breaks into excited chitter.

"Of course." I'm unable to hold back a smile. "Anything you want, love."

"I want that. So, Mother, if you want our line tied to Gentry Aspen so bad, you bond with him."

The queen narrows her eyes. "You know that's not possible."

"I do. So let it go." Ember claps her hands. "Now, is everyone done with this ridiculous game? I'm hungry and want my mate and his second to experience their first Seelie feast."

CHAPTER TWENTY-FIVE

EPILOGUE

EMBER

It's been seven moons since The Springfest Sprint. Never in my years did I expect my path to travel to this.

Donovan's fingers tighten in my hair, and I blink up at him, loving the heat in his gaze and the curl of his lips that show off his fangs. "You're going to make me come so hard, Princess." His eyes flutter closed when I point my tongue and slide it up the underside of his cock, bumping over his three piercings.

Auralia halts her talented tongue. "No, she's not, and you know it." At least she's talking to him. That's progress. "She only lets you have her during hunts."

She's correct. I enjoy teasing Donovan so much that most of our playtime is me pushing the limits of his patience. The sounds he makes when he's right on the edge and then I hold back are addictive.

He skims his fingers down my wings and lower. "Quiet, Aura." He pinches her nipple so hard, she squeals and lets out a string of curses.

I lean back, popping off of Donovan's length, and wiggle my hips over her face. "Yeah, Aura. Shush."

She claws my backside, dragging my center back down to her greedy mouth and tonguing me hard. *These two.*

I moan, and Donovan pulls me back to him, chest rising and falling with excited breathing. I open for him, and he slides his cock in until I nearly choke, smirking down at me before dropping his head back and making a guttural groan.

His fingers tighten again. "Yes. Keep going. Your mouth is so fucking hot, Princess." Just as Donovan picks up the pace, losing control, groaning on every exhale, Auralia sucks my clit.

I pop off of him with a gasp and sit up, rolling my hips, lost to the pleasure.

Donovan growls. "You're both demons." But he leans to kiss my parted lips and gently plucks my nipples, making the pleasurable ache tighten through me. "I want to fuck," he says against my lips.

"And you can."

I look behind me as Typhon pushes off the wall next to our open bedroom door.

"You're late," I moan as he shucks his clothing.

He steps next to the bed, grabbing my wrist and dragging me from Auralia just as the slightest flutters were beginning.

I growl, and so does Auralia. "I like her taste, Prince," Auralia seethes.

"As do I." Ty's voice is a rumbly grumble, and his eyes are bright red. I'm in for it. Possessive Typhon is a glorious thing.

I flip and attempt to crawl back toward Auralia just to push him further, but he drags me back by my wrist and ankle, opens me to him, and gives a long, slow lick between my legs that makes me mew and arch for him.

Upside down, I watch Donovan turn a dark gaze on Auralia. I'm not the only one in for it.

She's been particularly short with him lately, and he's back to avoiding her. Until today. I'd pat myself on the back, but Ty has my hands pinned.

Donovan flips her over and slaps her backside. "Be still while I take my pleasure from you."

She gasps, then narrows her eyes, but turns, hiding her smirk.

I'd love to watch this unfold, but Ty drags his fangs over my stomach, making me lose my mind. He twirls his tongue around my nipple. Just as I start to relax under his sweet touch, he jerks me to him, staring down at me. "You started without me, hellfire."

Tracing a circle around his nipple, I shrug. "The diplomarians kept you too long."

"I know." Ty runs claws down my side, sending a wave of chills over me. "You sent a note to tell me you were bored and naked. Which is why I arrived as soon as they approved the open gate to the spring fae's western border—"

"It's happening?" Having an open access route for trade and transport between our courts will change everything. Traveling by earth isn't nearly as easy as Ty makes it seem.

"Yes. We will bring your mother to meet the full board and approve everything tomorrow. But back to the important things. I come back to find you preoccupied." He slaps my breast, sending a jolt of pleasurable sting through my nipple. "Bad little fae."

I smile and push up to suck his lip. "It's because I know how much you enjoy interrupting, and I like it when you get all growly."

His throat vibrates.

I kiss it and moan. "And you like to get all growly." I grip his very firm cock and whisper in his ear, "And our lovers needed incentive."

He nods in understanding and glances past me to watch, but grips my neck when I try to watch, too. "Punishment," he whispers. "Fuck, that's hot."

Donovan hisses as Auralia keens and then muffles her voice, probably against a pillow. There's skin-to-skin slapping I need to see.

"Hey," I complain.

Ty smiles, and kisses me, then flips me over so I can watch their hard fucking, grips my hips, and thrusts in with no warning, making me cry out at the harsh taking. "You're mine, hellfire."

"I know, lover. And you're mine. Always."

"And forever," he murmurs, voice dark and rough with his fleeing patience. "My perfect little—"

"Stop being ridiculous, you two," Auralia mumbles. "I'm trying to concentrate on getting off over here."

Donovan grips her chin and turns her face toward him. "Then maybe concentrate on me instead of them."

"But they're so interesting."

Donovan's nostrils flare and he pulls from her, dragging her up and thrusting hard into her mouth. "What were you saying?"

Auralia glares and mumbles as Donovan smiles maliciously down at her. The tension in the room feels like it could crumble the stone walls.

Ty kisses between my wings and sets to a rhythm that makes my wings flutter.

That bond between us tightens, and I glance over my shoulder at my Unseelie's gorgeous face.

Who would have thought a Seelie tradition I was running from would bring me to my True Mate and open a world of opportunity for us?

NEXT UP...

Turn the page for a sneak peek of book 2, Auralia and Donovan's story,
Stealing the Bogeyman's Bride

Copyright © 2025 by Poppy Minnix

STEALING THE BOGEYMAN'S BRIDE

Chapter 1 - Love is Dumb

AURALIA

As first advisor to the missing king, I made an oath to represent the Unseelie Crown Court with grace and dignity. Yet, here I am, hiding behind a castle curtain.

My earlier argument with Donovan over how to address the on-going issue of our missing king got me worked up, and I might have flashed him as I stormed out of the meeting—subtly, of course. And then I've avoided him for the rest of the day, because I know better than to tease him. Or I don't, because I can't seem to stop.

Shame on me. Again.

From not far enough away, Jinora's tinkling laugh sounds more like a Seelie's, and I want to bite her tiny nose off.

His responding chuckle is carefree. Looks like she was available to soothe his irritation.

Clutching my shirt over my heart, I think about where he went since I toss him into a tornado of mixed signals daily.

Did they spend the day fucking their way through every position I know firsthand he's exceptional at? It's likely.

Did he look at her with sweetness? Carefully caress her because she's kind and gentle? Of course, he did.

I haven't experienced something like that with him. Frustrated moments of uncontainable lust make up our interactions, because I can't allow myself to fall further than I already have.

We've known of each other for a decade, but three rotations ago, I gave in to my wants and, unfortunately, being in bed—or against walls, doors, the castle wall, or behind curtains—with Donovan was far better than I'd expected. Ever since then, I've been fighting with myself to leave him be. Don't let him closer. *Don't put him in danger.*

Their muffled words sound like they're spoken against skin.

I dig my nails into my palms to distract myself from the images my brain supplies when I should conceptualize every detail of the perfect life Donovan and Jinora would have together. That is not our future, and I need to let him go. I need to get out of here before they wander even closer, and I overhear sweet words that will burn my charred heart further. He's not mine and never ever will be. *Stop this now, Auralia. Sneak away, go rescue your king and get back to upholding the will of the Unseelie Crown Court for as long as you can.*

Footsteps approach and an energy that is unmistakably Donovan's halts too close.

A shiver rolls up my spine.

The curtain opens with gusto.

Donovan's face is so beautiful. It's like looking into a perfect moon for too long and then being unable to see anything else in the darkness. With big brown eyes, dimples, and a square jaw—he's too much. His black curls look as if Jinora gave them a good tug when she came, and rage consumes me. However, his gaze is twinkling with mischief and I'm very busted. He knows me well—or as well as I've allowed him to know me.

I grip the curtain fabric to shake it. "These are getting dingy. You should see to the maintenance as the stand-in king's second."

"Are you so bored that you're insulting the decor, pet?"

He knows I hate that nickname so much, but not why. I'll never confess, but now it's a game to him—one I created by my reaction. And when he wants to taunt me, he knows how.

I bare my teeth at him. "Better than insulting your choice of bedmates. Don't you think, little Donnie?"

His eyes narrow and he steps close enough that I'm surrounded by the heat of his powerful body and the scent of berried wine and cacao.

My mouth waters. I slip to the side.

He flattens a palm against the wall, blocking me in. "Are you insulting yourself, Aura?" His purring tone calls right to my nipples and my wings go hot. He traces a line over the sensitive membrane with his finger and smirks.

"I'm not your bedmate." I duck and spin out of reach. Letting go of him is at the top of my priority list and yet, right before I dart around the corner, I glance back at him and my eyebrows raise in question without thought. Stupid me, pretending this is a game when it's not. Why do I do this to myself? To him? It's not fair to either of us, but my life hasn't been fair for eleven rotations, and my shame still feels fresh. I was so reckless and young. So needy and trusting.

Yet my past has taught me nothing because I stupidly love Donovan Germanthia with everything I am.

I'll never show him that. Never say it. I can't.

Because I stupidly loved someone else first, and I betrayed the Unseelie kingdom for him in the worst way.

ABOUT THE AUTHOR

POPPY MINNIX

Poppy Minnix is an award-winning author of mythology romantasy and contemporary romance. She loves to reimagine the world with ancient myths present, then dash in some spice and humor. Her characters are hot messes who find their perfect fit in life and in romance. You will find an escape, hidden strength, intriguing and diverse characters, and overcoming shame or guilt in her books.

She lives in Maryland with a husband who is far more romantic than she is, kids, pets, and plants—everything she immensely loves.

Find more about her on socials and her newsletter.

Poppy Minnix
www.poppyminnix.com
poppymwrites@gmail.com

ACKNOWLEDGMENTS

Huge thanks to my kind Vella readers who wanted this to be in novelette form so they could gobble it down in one sitting!

My writer friends Lara, Kristin, Kristen, and Rebecca! Thanks for the sprints, pokes, and help with that pesky blurb. You all rock and I'm thrilled to have met you!

To my family—thanks for being patient while I write one more word (or paragraph or chapter—whatever, you know me). The world would have a lot more art if every creative had constant support and love like you give me.